D1505030

To my family, who have supported my voice and nurtured me to be brave

R.D.

Viva's Voice is published by
Kind World Publishing, PO Box 22356, Eagan, MN 55122
www.kindworldpublishing.com

Text copyright © 2022 by Raquel Donoso
Illustrations copyright © 2022 by Carlos Vélez
Cover and book design by Tim Palin Creative

Kind World Publishing supports copyright, free speech, and the vibrant culture that their protection encourages. All rights of this work are reserved. No part of this publication may be reproduced in whole or in part in any manner whatsoever nor transmitted in any form or by any means whatsoever without the prior written permission of Kind World Publishing and Consulting, LLC, except for the inclusion of brief quotations in an acknowledged review.

Published in 2022 by Kind World Publishing.

Printed in the United States of America.

ISBN 978-1-63894-006-7 (hardcover)
ISBN 978-1-63894-011-1 (ebook)

Library of Congress Control Number: 2022933939

VIVA'S VOICE

by
Raquel Donoso
illustrated by
Carlos Vélez

Kind
World
PUBLISHING
Eagan, Minnesota

Since the day she was born, Viva's voice had been the mightiest in the room.

It boomed like an earthquake.

It shook the slide on the playground.

But it was especially loud at home, always overpowering Papi's quiet voice.

Papi's voice was quiet, but his job was loud. Papi drove buses. Very BIG, very LOUD buses. Two buses actually connected to make one GIANT snake, swerving and curling through town.

Viva loved riding around town with Papi on his bus, greeting passengers along the way. "HOLA!" she would yell as they got on the bus.

And "HASTA LUEGO!" as they climbed off.

The sounds of the cars. HONK! HONK!

The bus doors opening and closing. WHOOSH! THUD!

All of it was music to Viva's ears.

And the tacos, quesadillas, and hot chocolate they stopped for were music to Viva's tummy.

Today was Viva's first day of summer break,
and she couldn't wait to spend the day with Papi.

"Papi, I'm ready to go to work with you today!" Viva shouted,
jumping up and down.

"Mija, not today," Papi murmured.

"Viva, please don't bother Papi today," said Mami.

"But why?"

"I'm on strike and not sure when I'll go back to driving buses."
Papi spoke softly.

"What's a strike?" asked Viva, raising her eyebrow and wrinkling her nose.

"I'm a part of a group of people called a union," Papi explained. "Unions help workers get treated fairly. The bus drivers want more pay and better benefits. We have decided to stop working and go on strike until we get the things we asked for."

"What do you do on a strike?" Viva wondered.

"We go to the offices where our bosses work and hold up signs and chant. That's called a picket line. We let everyone know what we want. One voice alone may not be heard. But lots of voices together can make a big noise."

"Papi, I can strike!" Viva exclaimed. "I know how to make lots of noise."

"Oh, I know you do, Viva. But this isn't a place for little kids," Papi said.

Viva hated to be told she couldn't do something because she was little.

"Por favor, Papi. I promise to listen to you and be quiet. Plllleeeeaaassse," implored Viva.

"Remember, I'm working early today," added Mami.

"Well," Papi said, "I guess that means you're coming with me."

The picket line was magical.

Signs bounced up and down, bright blue and red.

Cars passed by, honking their horns.

A woman with a bullhorn chanted questions and everyone in the crowd responded.

It was music to Viva's ears.

Viva learned the responses quickly and delighted in shouting along with everyone else.

She was sure today was the very best first day of summer break ever, until she looked at Papi.

"What's wrong, Papi?" asked Viva, seeing his furrowed forehead.

"I have to go on stage and make a speech in front of all those people," he admitted in his quiet voice.

He didn't talk much and he definitely didn't like to yell. Even when Viva did something wrong, Papi never raised his voice.

"Papi, I'll go up with you," Viva offered, squeezing his hand.

Papi let out a long, deep exhale. His forehead relaxed.

With Viva nearby, Papi found the courage to belt out his speech. The crowd's chants got louder and louder. Everyone was cheering them on.

Papi put Viva on his shoulders and handed her the bullhorn.

"¡Sí, se puede! ¡Sí, se puede!" she shouted to the cheering crowd.

On the drive home, Viva honked Papi's horn.

The faint chants of the workers on the picket line echoed in her ears.

"Viva, your voice made me brave today. I wouldn't have had the courage to give that speech without you," Papi said.

Viva smiled. Papi's words were music to her ears.

DEAR READER,

Viva's story is based on my own experience going to the picket line with my dad as a little girl. He was a bus driver for the city of Los Angeles. My mom, my sister, my brother, and I would ride with him sometimes when he worked on weekends. We loved it!

Several times during my childhood, the bus drivers went on strike. They wanted better pay and benefits. It was hard for our family during these times.

When my dad took me to the picket line, I loved the energy, the songs, and the people speaking up. I felt like we were doing something important. That experience inspired me to be active in my community and speak up for things that matter to me.

RAQUEL

Labor unions are groups of workers who come together to protect workers' rights by negotiating with employers. A strike is when members of a labor union stop working, usually because the workers want better pay and working conditions.

One of the first labor unions in the United States was started by shoemakers in the 1700s. And tailors protesting a wage reduction launched one of the first worker strikes. Over the years, unions have been key to protecting workers' rights, such as shorter work hours and breaks, health insurance, and workers getting paid when they cannot work because of illness or injuries received on the job. Unions even supported laws about children going to school instead of being forced to work.

Unions still exist today. Teachers, firefighters, nurses, and even professional athletes have unions.

What is something you or your family might go on strike for?

Some workers' rights include having time for breaks and being paid well. What other kinds of rights do you think workers should have?

TALK ABOUT IT

When you feel afraid, how do you make yourself feel brave?

How do members of your family support you when you feel scared or nervous?

How do you support members of your family when they need it?

Viva loves riding the bus and going to the picket line with her Papi. What do you love to do with the adults in your life? How do they make you feel?

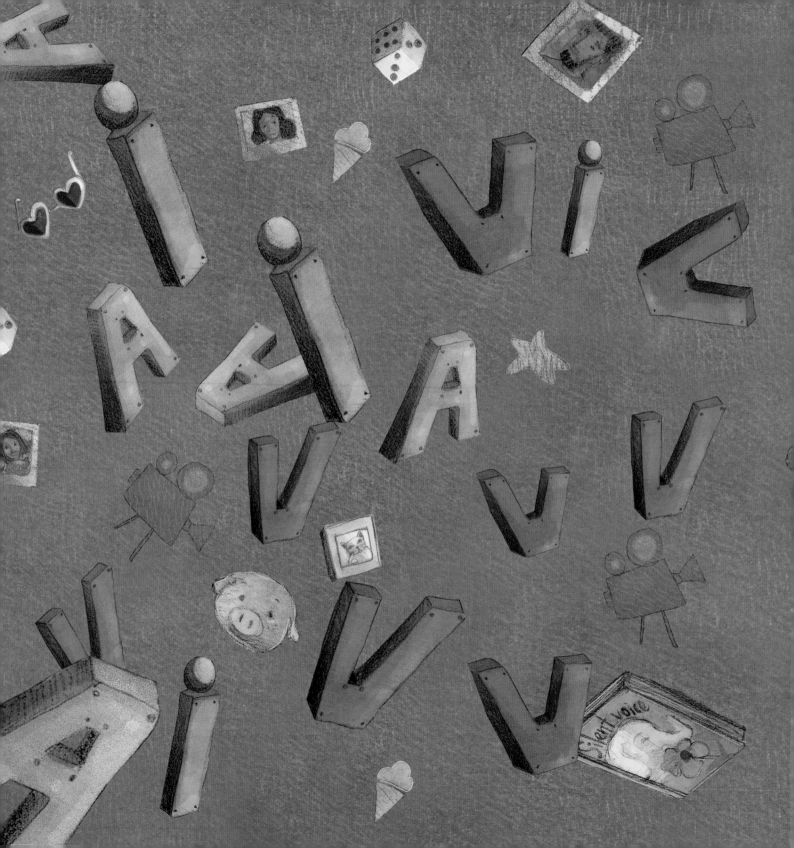